Considerations

Considerations

Hubert van Zeller

SHEED AND WARD · LONDON

FOR MOTHER PERPETUA

First published 1973, this edition 1974

Nihil obstat Francis Bartlett, Censor
Imprimatur David Norris, Vicar General, Westminster, 12 August 1974
This book is printed in Great Britain for
Sheed and Ward Limited,
6 Blenheim St, London W1Y 0SA
by Redwood Burn Limited, Trowbridge & Esher

Contents

PREFACE

Considerations is not running in competition with Pascal's *Pensees*, Hammarskjold's *Markings*, or *Thoughts of Chairman Mao.* In spite of this disclaimer, however, it is idle to expect that the writer will escape the charge of pretension. The impression produced by the book's layout as much as by the text will be of an author who will be seen wearing the smug look of one who has lingered among the mysteries of human existence, who has pondered upon the facets of truth, who has at last found himself and can now put at the disposal of mankind a sort of spiritual and psychological ready-reckoner. Correcting this idea of sureness and security, it may be said that far from having discovered the universal panacea, the author submits nothing but the fruit, some of it unripe and some of it stale, of a lifetime's guessing, fumbling, faltering, asking questions to which there were no answers, sailing seas to which there was no port, mugging up the theory and misapplying it in practice, letting go and taking hold again, seeing neither the wood nor the trees, and ending up hoping for the best. What follow are reflections only, not unassailable conclusions. Many of them are reflections upon the current mood, and it is worth noting that climates of change produce their own uncertainties.

Perhaps what has been selected reflects a too individualistic examination and argument: a logic to which most would not subscribe and an experience which many would not have shared. But if it were otherwise, what would be the point? If it reflected only the opinions and searchings of other men, why not let the classical authorities have their say and keep one's mouth shut? Whether too personal or too sweeping, whether axe-grinding or in the abstract, whether oblique or self-evident, the observations which follow are submitted seriously, humbly, sincerely. This, and not their spiritual insight, is their sole justification.

THE WORLD AND I

When a man tells you the world holds no attraction for him you know that he is either completely insensitive or a liar.

———

Some people are by nature more worldly than others but even the most spiritual have a streak of worldliness in them. Without such a streak they could hardly make allowances for the worldly.

———

It is not because worldliness is no temptation to them that people are classified as unworldly. It is because by grace and self-denial they have come to live in the world of the spirit.

———

"The wisdom of the world" St. Paul says, "is death." This would imply that the so-called worldly wise are dead or dying. What St. Paul means by being wise in the ways of the world is not merely making calculated judgments but making the calculated choice: this world at the price of the next. And this *is* death.

———

The conjunction "the world, the flesh, the devil" suggests images of extravagance and abandon: the roulette table, the champagne bucket, fast cars and nightclub life. But the world is more subtle, the flesh more constant, the devil more astute.

———

There are as many worlds within the one world as there are personal attractions within the one person. The worldly are those who allow their attractions to focus on material things and values. The worldly man turns his desires in the wrong direction and gives them freedom of operation.

——————

I can be worldly without necessarily being self-indulgent. But I cannot be consistently self-indulgent without being worldly.

——————

Provided I make Christ's life my own I am not likely to be seduced by the world. Christ was not seduced by the world or the devil or the flesh. But he was exposed, as I am, to temptation from all three.

——————

At the end of his forty days' fast our Lord was tempted in an ascending scale of significance: body, vanity, pride and ambition. The temptations amount to one temptation: the world against the spirit.

——————

If the world presented a clear-cut option we would be on our guard. The warning light would shine, and we would pray and wait for the temptation to pass. But worldliness disguises itself as the rational and begs us to be reasonable.

——————

The trouble about falling in with "a little harmless worldliness for once" is that the outlines of worldliness become rapidly indistinct. Before I know what is happening I am as worldly as those who have never been anything else.

I may tell myself that in order to win the worldly I must avoid being too unworldly. It is in the interests of the world to set off a whole series of such fallacies. Yet if I make an idol of my unworldliness I help nobody, either directly or indirectly, and least of all myself.

———

In justifying itself the world argues cogently. "If God had meant you to resist the world," a worldly man tells me, "why did he place you in it?" "If you are to help the world" he says, "you should accept its terms and show you understand its problems." "The way to the Creator" he urges, "is through his creatures." Truth and fallacy mixed.

———

The contrast could not be sharper. Thinking with the world blunts the conscience, confuses the judgment, substitutes one lot of values for another. Thinking in the spirit sharpens sensitivity, appreciates the priorities, exposes deceits, laughs at anomalies. The world is a dead end, the spirit gives life.

———

Worldliness corrupts and absolute worldliness corrupts absolutely. But it is not something invented by the affluent society. It goes back to the Garden of Eden. The material thing is given first place.

———

In our egalitarian age snobbishness is taken to be the crime before all others. But snobbishness is only a very superficial expression of worldliness. When class distinctions are ironed out and all men are equal, worldliness will be the same as it ever was. So also, but of another kind, will snobbishness.

Simon, the pharisee who entertained our Lord at dinner, was a snob. But it was his worldliness as much as his snobbishness which caused him to neglect the courtesies due to a guest.

———

Primitive Christianity, as described in the Acts, broke free from the materialism of the time and so, for an all too brief period, conquered the world. It could be done again if our Lord's words were taken literally.

———

Again and again attempts have been made, in pre-Christian as well as in Christian times, to practice an unworldly way of life. Always it has been the few who have preached such detachment. Minorities count before God but they do not cut much ice in the eyes of the world.

———

St. Paul warns the Corinthians against letting their ideals corrode, allowing them to be "turned away from the simplicity that is in Christ". The spirit makes for unity, the world for multiplicity.

———

The world preaches the love of life and accordingly loses it; Christ preaches the losing of life which accordingly finds it. Everywhere the same paradox. The one seed doing all in its power to live and succeeding only in wasting itself; the other dying and giving life.

———

The world expresses itself in magnificence, the spirit in magnaminity. The one means making big, inflating. The other means greatness (or openness) of mind, heart, soul. It is the difference between false and true generosity.

The world has a funny idea of generosity. It buys a stretch of river so as to provide salmon for the peasantry (who can get salmon anyway by poaching). It lands on a slum playground in a helicopter and gives out Christmas trees (to people who would rather have the money to buy food). The world laughs at bread but takes *pate de foie gras* seriously.

The world has a funny idea of religious worship. It does not worship in order to praise God but in order to entertain itself. Religious services have to be made attractive, have to show originality, have to be startling and unexpected. God does not delight in novelty, and if worship is not meant to delight God then why worship?

The world has a funny idea of community. If its "togetherness" means nothing more than being sociable there is little to keep it together. Community means charity or it is nothing.

Worldly people harden under adversity; unworldly people, more ready to accept, become more flexible. The world does not like being shaped according to God's plan; the spirit does.

If he gives himself a chance of thinking seriously, the sane man will admit that the only things really worth pursuing in this life are the things of God. The worldly man may not deny this but he lives as though he does.

———

"Pride makes a man almost insane" St. Bonaventure claims, "for it teaches him to despise what is most precious and esteem what is most contemptible." Pride and worldliness share this insanity.

———

St. Paul has the answer to our weakness for worldliness where he says that we must "care for the things that are above, not the things that are upon the earth". But we have heard this doctrine so often that we do not pay it much attention.

———

As if the teaching of unworldliness were not enough we have the example of the saints. St. Norbert, when he came to take possession of the episcopal see to which he was appointed, was turned away from the back door as being an undesirable vagrant. When the cardinal's hat was brought by papal messengers to St. Bonaventure it was left on a shrub in the garden until the saint had finished washing the dishes in the kitchen.

TEMPERAMENT AND CHARACTER

Temperament is what you are born with. Character is what you make of it.

———

Childhood reveals tendencies. Youth develops personality. Maturity establishes character.

———

You cannot escape influences. They are there for you to allow or refuse, choose or reject. What you decide about them will determine your character. "A man is what he chooses" says St. Augustine.

———

Friends, suffering, marriage, environment, study and recreation are influences which shape character. The strongest influence, if you are generous enough to yield to it, is the grace of God.

———

The church and the sacraments exist to rescue character and bring out the best in it. Christ did this during his lifetime and has been doing it ever since.

———

Character is not formed by dreams but by ideals. Dreams in fact can weaken character. Nightmares can weaken it even more.

To some people dreams may become more real than realities. But this does not mean that dreams to them *are* realities, *are* fact, *are* the stuff of everyday life.

——————

Any substitute for truth can be fatal to character. The substitute can come to be his gospel which he will defend in the spirit of a Christian martyr.

——————

The man who is afraid of truth and its implications will tell you that what the gospel holds out is a dream, and that he prefers to be realistic rather than to live in any airy world of fancy. He has mistaken aspiration for imagination.

——————

A man may think of himself as a good or bad character, and this will to a large extent determine his action. It is better not to think of himself as either.

——————

People too easily equate forcefulness, and the ability to make quick decisions, with character. Even having high principles is not an infallible sign of character. The young man in the gospel who agreed to do his father's will evidently had high principles about obedience, but it was the other son who showed character.

——————

Character is not abiding firmly to a course. If the course is seen to be the wrong one, it shows far more character to go back on what was either a too precipitate decision or a decision based on wrong information.

Only when they are inspired by high ideals are fixed principles indicative of character. Ideals shape principles, principles dictate standards, and conforming to standards makes for character.

Hero-worship, associated with the young and impressionable but common enough in later life, can affect character more than is generally supposed. Worship of any sort affects character, whether of God, a cause, a hero.

The drawback to hero-worship is that it can drain away the worshipper's personality, substituting one character for another. New lamps for old; and it is possible that there is more light in the old.

No human being is meant to be a carbon copy, a double, an understudy, a *doppelganger*, a shadow. Each must be his own man, much as this may mean resembling someone else's. This is not egocentricity or independence of the herd. It is the incommunicable response to the particular summons of God.

When a man genuinely and humbly feels he has discovered the buried treasure of the gospel he naturally wants to spread the good news to others and so to bring them closer to God. He must be on his guard, however, not to let them stop short at himself.

People of zeal and forceful character can do harm by wanting to impose their zeal and character on others. God wants people formed in his own image, not in mine. I may not put my signature to a masterpiece of God's.

Though acting with the best will in the world the would-be reformer should remember how the human character works. To want to be loved is natural, to want to be improved is less so, to want to be reformed is very unusual indeed.

The greatest mistake about our own character is to imagine that we can do nothing to strengthen it. We have the gift of free will, and every day of our lives we are using it either to build up or pull down. My mind is not an inert substance which has no power of self-direction. God does not wish me simply to lie there and leave everything to him.

LONELINESS AND SOLITUDE

Being at home is not necessarily connected with being in a place you have chosen or been brought up in. Neither does it lie in doing a work which suits you. Not even is it living in a family which depends on you and on which you depend. Home is being able to leave and return without agonizing over either and being content about both.

———

Until a man knows that he belongs, and knows too that he can go on belonging, he will not enjoy peace. He will be alone wherever he is and whatever he is doing. Whether in company or in solitude he will feel he belongs somewhere else. He will be restless. He will attribute his loneliness to being in the wrong environment. But the matter goes deeper than this.

———

Peace and the sense of belonging may not be the same thing, but for the possession of one there has to be a large measure of the other. Certain it is that neither is likely to be lasting unless there is a conviction that mood has as little to do with it as locality, money, age or health. Neither contentment on the one hand or loneliness on the other is determined by these things.

———

The man of moods, even if his good moods outlast his bad, is a lonely man. When in a good mood he will forget that he has ever been lonely, and when in a bad mood he will think he has never been anything else. Loneliness is something which has got to be kept under constant control, and nothing more surely disposes for the grace of serenity than a calculated indifference to variations of mood.

If a man is not sure of his direction he is unsure of himself. He is lonely because he is on his own, and at every step he has to guess. But even the loneliness of insecurity can be met and transcended. So long as the man who gropes by guesswork can make the act of trust in God, and try to mean it though his feelings tell him he is not meaning it, he is in the right direction whether he knows it or not.

That Jesus was lonely is indisputable. Not only during his agony in the garden when his friends failed him, not only at every stage of his passion when again he had to endure his sufferings alone, not only when on the cross and he felt himself to be deserted by his Father, but also throughout his life when he looked for understanding and hardly ever met with it. If he allowed loneliness to be his lot, was it not to invite the lonely to unite their lot with his?

Essentially loneliness is the knowledge that one's fellow human beings are incapable of understanding one's condition and therefore are incapable of bringing the help most needed. It is not a question of companionship – many are ready to offer this and companionship is certainly not to be despised – but rather one of strictly sharing, of identifying. No two human beings can manage this, so to a varying extent loneliness at times is the lot of all.

Allowing the existence of a gulf which necessarily exists between every other human being and myself, I have still the unifying element of grace to draw upon. If I cannot sublimate my loneliness at a natural level, I can still transcend it at a supernatural level. By God's grace I can live in that dimension of faith which puts human loneliness in eclipse. The companionship of Christ, not appreciated by the senses in the way that human companionship is, can become such an abiding reality in my life that loneliness at the human level is a small price to pay for it. Faith can take the place of feeling, and faith is unifying.

———

Loneliness and fear go together, and if love can cast out fear it can do the same with loneliness. Yet experience shows that our love is seldom perfect enough to do more than temporarily suspend our fear and loneliness. In proportion as our imperfect love is purified our tendency to fear, doubt, worry and be lonely will be lessened. Where faith and love take over there is little room for dread and the sense of alienation.

———

What do I dread most? The answer nearly always is having to face this or that ordeal alone. It is being cut off. It is not the ordeal itself; it is the being with it on my own. Death is one such ordeal. Not the moment or the pain, but the being out of reach.

———

Unless I come to terms with loneliness I make death more menacing than it need be. Indeed I make life more menacing than it need be. Lacking help from without and confidence from within, I shall shrink from every crisis in my life. Inevitably the crisis of death will be dreaded above all others.

———

Afraid of losing what little security I can count upon, I shall not dare to break out from the ring of experience safely tried. My fear of loneliness not only robs me of confidence in my relations with others but eats away at the very security which I am trying to safeguard.

It is the dread of alienation which alienates. Within my supposedly sheltering walls I shall become more and more lonely, more and more afraid, less and less open to the liberating influence of grace.

———

Just as fear unchecked increases the capacity for fear, so loneliness unchecked increases the tendency to be lonely. A man begins to doubt, and ends up without any certainties whatever. Just as love and faith are the only antidote to fear and loneliness, so the same virtues must be brought to bear upon uncertainty, evasion of life, insecurity, the longing to bury one's head in the sand and let the world go by.

———

Doubt, like loneliness for which it is often responsible, would be endurable if someone could only see into our minds and help us towards certainty. But though all of us are more or less doubters, each of us stands alone with his doubt.

———

You would think that if lonely people came together they would be company for one another and would lose their loneliness. Sometimes this in fact happens, and those to whom it happens should be grateful for their good fortune. But you have only to visit an old folks' home to see how this coming together can lead to further isolation, to an interior alienation which forbids communication.

———

The world is full of people who are haunted by their sense of inadequacy. The world is full of people who are haunted, and this is more serious, by their sense of guilt. The fear that they will never be reassured drives them to one of two alternatives: either they take refuge in a solitude which shows up their inadequacy all the more clearly or they try to escape into the kind of distractions which only increase their sense of guilt.

———

It is the psychiatrist's job to tell me I am as adequate as the next man. But do I believe him? How can he possibly know? Is there a standard of adequacy against which my performance can be measured? I leave the psychiatrist for the priest. It is the priest's job to tell me I am forgiven and must not feel guilty any longer. Though I can bring myself to believe I am forgiven, I go on feeling guilty all the same. "You must trust more" the priest says, "and as things now stand you are innocent." Shame tells me I am far from innocent. My guilty life is spent among innocents. Interiorly I am an outcast, an exile. So of course I am lonely.

———

Loneliness is not simply a matter of finding myself spiritually and socially on a desert island. It is more a matter of wanting to reach out to other people and being unable to. It is wanting to be reached out to and knowing that this can never satisfactorily happen. At the spiritual level it is wanting to reach out to God and not knowing how to. It is wanting him to reach out to me and feeling that he is never likely to.

———

Sheer physical solitude can in some cases, by adroit planning, be avoided. What cannot be avoided is the solitude within oneself. The only way of not dreading either of these solitudes is to deepen one's faith in the presence of Christ.

———

When the implications of Christ's presence are understood — both his presence in the outside world and in the intimacy of the human soul – then guilt, fear, doubt, disappointment, worry and regret will have less hold. They will go on presenting themselves but with a difference.

———

Such human ills, and other horrors besides, will be seen as shadows and not as substances. Always there will be the presence of Christ to put them in the context of his passion. Christ's sufferings are substance, ours are shadow. Christ is the Word; we are the echo from the text. We could not be accorded a higher dignity.

———

Once I have grasped the doctrine of God's presence, which means nothing less than the indwelling of the Blessed Trinity, I can no longer be obsessed with the fear of being alone with my guilt. Assuming I do not spoil everything by deliberately abandoning God, I am not alone and never need be.

———

Only when it is an indulgence like any other does the gift of solitude have to be questioned. Not necessarily to be renounced out of hand but to be held up to the light. God lets us know soon enough if our love for solitude is an exaggeration, an affectation, an excuse for getting out of work and for denying the claims of charity.

———

Some would hold that solitude can take the place of prayer. Thus it is claimed that since in solitude as in prayer the soul is, in a way not otherwise experienced, up against reality and exposed to the most searching light of grace, a man may hang about in solitude and not bother to pray. Solitude is not itself praise, witness, gratitude, love. It may provide the best conditions for prayer but it is not prayer. Solitude is to prayer what acoustics are to a concert. You can get the acoustics right but you will still need the music.

It is in order to worship more perfectly that people seek solitude and are prepared to put up with its loneliness. If the solitude which they find is not love, then it is emptiness.

If the lonely do not utilize their loneliness, making it serve in the worship of God, then it is not only an opportunity wasted but a distraction to the worship of God.

Emptiness does not remain empty indefinitely. If it does not fill up with God it fills up with self. Nature is not the only one who abhors a vacuum. God does the same. Grace rejected is grace put in reverse.

Loneliness and solitude rightly directed must significantly influence the life of prayer. In this combined element the soul learns. The interior sensibilities are heightened. More of truth reveals itself. The perspectives become clearer. There is no longer the fear of being left alone.

We are always being told that no man is an island, but are not most of us islands? Desert islands at that. Each man has his empty shore of sand, his jungle thicket, his struggle for survival. Left to himself he deals with whatever habitation there is as best he can. But the point is that if he has faith in the presence and providence of God he is not left to himself.

Meeting the demands of his God-ordered condition, a man can come to value the vocation of castaway. Without self-pity, cynicism or dramatization, he will find a peace which he did not find when living among people. To be solitary, to be able to breathe at the soul's instance, will become to him more desirable than anything else in the world.

HAPPINESS AND UNHAPPINESS

From the endless talk that goes on about happiness you come to equate it with peace and contentment. You are probably right. Though few can lay claim to possessing them, all remain aware of having fleetingly experienced these qualities. This leads people to hope that they will experience them again. Without such hope the world would destroy itself.

———

In moments of great happiness, and contributing largely to the feeling of it, there is the conviction that the memory of this present experience will bring joy. The exact reverse may be the case.

———

Since the material is already present, happiness and unhappiness are not what we make them but what we make *of* them. A determination to develop our potential unhappiness brings its own inevitable result. The determination to be happy is not so certain in effect but at least it is a good start.

———

More people are destroyed by unhappiness than by drink, drugs, disease, or even failure. There must be something about sadness which attracts or people would not accept it so readily into their lives.

———

Poverty, old age, sickness, exile: these things are conditions. Sadness is a state of mind. Conditions may not always be improved upon but states of mind usually can be.

Man's instinctive straining towards happiness is as natural as a bubble of air under water straining towards the surface. The curious thing is that when man reaches the surface he does not know where to look or what to do next.

———

An unhappy man is nearly always one who is at the mercy of some greed or some fear. Weighed down by selfish desire or dread, or both, he is not giving himself room to lead the life he is meant to live. The wish to escape occupies him to the exclusion of all else.

———

People talk about restlessness as though outward conditions were responsible for it. The reason why we are restless is that we have refused to accept and have allowed imagined environments to call the tune. This is something essentially inward.

———

The tragedy about people who cannot settle and be happy is that, having projected themselves into one role after another, they finally project themselves into the role of the unhappy. Restless still, they cast themselves as misfits. Defeatism brings its own sour satisfaction.

———

A man who is not at peace within himself is pulled in opposite directions. He wants to be independent of existing circumstances and he wants existing circumstances to bow to his wishes.

———

An obstacle to happiness, but one which can be overcome where there is humility, is the sense of inferiority. Self-assertion is no remedy but only an exercise in compensation.

Believing that he is marked down for failure, that he has not got a chance, that he is good for only bumpkin occupations anyway, a man can lose not only his self-respect but his right to happiness. Exaggerated humility is no humility. True humility is accompanied by a confidence which leapfrogs unhappiness.

———

If we made God's interests more vital than our own we would worry less about whether we were happy or unhappy. Christ tells us we are to lose our life if we are to find it. If we put our own life first we lose the happiness that is meant to go with it.

———

We know that if we examine our happiness too closely we lose it. But if we examine our unhappiness too closely we add to it.

———

It is right to look for satisfaction in work, in service of others, in affection, in religion. But to think too much about the happiness to which these things entitle us — or so we believe — is a mistake.

———

A man may be right or wrong about what he thinks he can most profitably do with his life. He will be less unhappy if he takes his chance and fails than if he is denied his chance and has to wait. It is impossible to be happy not knowing, not having proved anything, not seeing any likelihood of his hope being realized.

———

Obviously if we worried more about other people's happiness and unhappiness we would worry less about our own. But it is not simply a question of leaving no room, no time over, to attend to our own concerns. It is a question of charity and compassion: these are qualities which overflow, bringing back to us their own satisfactions.

———

One person can try to make another person happy. Strictly speaking it is the Christian duty of every person to try to make every other person happy. If people made use of their opportunity here the general level of happiness would inevitably be higher than it is.

———

Happiness is not like a suit made to measure, and which accordingly can be expected to fit. It is something inside a man or it is nowhere. He it is who is expected to do the fitting.

SANCTIFICATION AND CHRIST

No virtue is of any value to the Christian unless it partakes of the virtue of Christ. We cannot sanctify ourselves. We can ask to be sanctified but it is Christ who does the work. It is because of his grace that we are prompted to ask in the first place.

———

"You have not chosen me" our Lord reminds us "but I have chosen you." Having chosen us, he shows himself to be the way, the truth, and the life. Unless we are put on the way we founder. Unless we look for the truth we are caught up in lies. Unless we live in Christ we die.

———

Life in Christ is the Christian's sole title to completeness. If I am to be a whole man I must open myself to the whole Christ. I need to define my ethic. I need to proclaim my allegiance. I need to give direction to my conduct. Only in Christ do I find meaning and reality.

———

If I could know the mind of Christ on every issue with which I am faced I would have only the problem of how to put that knowledge into effect. But I do not invariably know so I have to make do by wanting to know. It is this wanting to know that signifies.

———

If I could find Christ in my prayer whenever I wanted to I would have no difficulty in praying. But I cannot invariably find him so I have to make do by searching for him. It is this search that signifies.

If I could see Christ in others – present there as my faith tells me he is – I would surely manage to be compassionate, patient, kind, considerate, long-suffering, tolerant – all the other enviable aspects of charity. It is trying to get behind the mask presented that signifies.

———

The older I get the more I am reminded, when I see strangers passing in the street, of people I have known long ago. Equally they should remind me of Christ to whom they bear an even closer likeness.

———

Standing in front of a shop window what do I see? The glass? The goods behind the glass? The raindrops on the glass? The people moving about beyond the glass? Probably I give most attention to my reflection in the glass. So it all depends what I want to see. Sanctity is like that.

———

"God so loved the world as to send his son into the world." Only by passing through the channel between God and the world can man's salvation be brought about. It is a two-way movement: Christ coming down to man and man taken up by Christ to God.

———

Nothing so effectively blocks communication between God and the soul as the dead weight of preoccupation with self. Sin blocks the way to and from God, but then sin is an aspect – the more manifestly reprehensible aspect – of preoccupation with self.

———

Our relationship with superiors and subjects alike is poisoned by maneuvering ourselves into positions, drawing attention to ourselves, striking attitudes. Self is interrupting the flow of grace through us to others and through others to us.

——————

Sanctity is not an end in itself but the means of giving greater glory to God. If we think of it as an achievement in its own right, an ambition realized, we forget its essential destination.

——————

Christ could say "I sanctify myself" because he was God, and God holds the prerogative of sanctity. Only in an analagous sense can we say that we are sanctifying ourselves. All we can do is to put ourselves into the disposition. Sanctity is what we allow God to do in us. While possessing the monopoly he excludes none from its enjoyment.

——————

"You must be holy" says God through the mouth of his prophet, "because I the Lord am holy." That, in case we should wonder why, is the reason. He does not say "because you are innocent, because you are intelligent, because you are eloquent, because I know you will put up with hardship for my sake and because you are humble and patient and industrious." He says "because *I*, the Lord, am holy."

——————

Even when the marks of it are patently obvious to other people, holiness is not something which the saint sees in himself. It is something he sees by. His prayer and charity give him the right perspectives.

——————

While people readily appreciate the harm which earthly desires can do to a man's spiritual progress they are not so sure about cares and worries. Might not anxious care be the sign of the perfectionist, legitimate worry the sign of the conscientious worker? We are talking about nervous apprehension. This is fear, and fear eats away at the spiritual life.

The soul who truly trusts cannot truly fear. The moment he begins to be afraid he will begin to show his trust. His confidence in God is greater than his dread.

Grace, perseverance, sanctification, salvation: these are God's gifts to man. While man has no right to anything he should know that all are his for the asking. What God wants in return is fidelity, and even this is impossible to man without God's help.

The moment a man starts aiming at the heights he casts about for a formula that will get him there. Each of his guides will come up with a new formula. In the end he will know that no one formula exists, and that he must work his way up the climb by love. Which is of course the formula.

People are inclined to identify holiness with suffering. Suffering may be its inseparable companion but it is not holiness. Suffering may be a contributing cause but it is not holiness. Holiness offers suffering to God whereas suffering cannot be so sure of offering holiness.

Sanctity is not getting noticeably nicer as you go along. It is a revolution. It is a continuous conversion.

Sanctity's *metonia*, the change of heart and mind, supposes a dynamic of grace and purpose. Mistakenly we think of it primarily as a dynamic of renunciation and action.

———

Renunciation and action perform a necessary function in sanctity, but not the primary function. Conversion *from* is half the battle; conversion *to* is the whole of it.

———

What God looks for is the soul's orientation: the doing for him what otherwise would be done for relative ends or for self.

———

You do not change the house to find sanctity. You change man inside the house to find sanctity. It is not the hermit's hood that matters; it is the head inside the hood that matters.

———

Sanctity is always choosing the will of God, and always choosing the will of God is sanctity. That's all ye know and all ye need to know. Amen.

JOY, DEATH, HEAVEN

St. Paul told the Galatians that "the fruit of the spirit is charity, joy, peace." In the liturgy we pray that "our hearts be set where true joys await us." The first quotation considers joy in this life, the second supposes the crowning of a joy which is necessarily unfulfilled and intermediate.

———

It is a mistake to think of heaven as one would think of a wonder-drug, which enables us to live here below in a state of holy optimism, and which finds verification in a state of euphoria which will last forever. Heaven is life in Christ fully realized, a sharing of his infinite joy.

———

While we cannot in this life enjoy all that our Lord came on earth to give – we need a heaven in which to experience it – we can anticipate in faith what we cannot appreciate in fact. Is not this itself a joy?

———

Though hope and prayer are not tricks to enable us to meet the hazards of life head on, they teach us the truth that God never allows our sufferings to be more than we can bear. If this does not amount to a joy what does?

———

Turning in contemplation to the gods, Socrates held, enables a man "to look death in the face with joyful hope and to consider this lasting truth: the righteous man has nothing to fear, neither in life nor in death, for the gods will not abandon him." In the Christian context, indeed in the context of any religion, this exactly expresses the point.

Although our time on earth is meant to be a preparation for it, heaven is seldom a topic of conversation. You would think we would be talking of little else.

———

"Seek the things that are above" St. Paul tells the Colossians, "where Christ is sitting at God's right hand." If we obeyed this exhortation we would be able to echo St. Ignatius: "How vile earth seems when I look up to heaven."

———

To those who are granted to live in the thought of eternity it should not be too difficult to meet one thing after another in time. A meal of crusts is satisfactory enough when you know that the next meal will be a proper one.

———

Only when you have not submitted to life as handed to you by the providence of God need the thought of death discourage. Instinctively you know that if you cannot accept the life God sends, neither will you accept the death he sends. The two go together.

———

Nathaniel West admitted that his life was overcast by the comparison between what life is and what it ought to be. But is not everyone's? "I am" he wrote, "one of the great despisers whom Nietzsche loved because they are the great adorers: they are arrows of longing for the other shore."

———

Naturally cheerful people are forever telling the naturally sad that there is never any reason to be sad. But if reasons are to be dragged in there is never any reason to be happy either.

Happiness and unhappiness do not depend on reasons but on the use made of the opportunities of God's grace.

———

"Ask and you shall receive" promises our Lord, "and so your joy will be complete." We do well to ask for joy, but it must be his before it is ours. "The joy of the Lord is your strength" we read in Nehemias. The joy that we look for apart from his can only be our weakness.

LIBERTY AND LAW

St. Augustine's "Love and do what you will" is offset by our Lord's "If you love me, keep my commandments." Only when we are ready to obey his commandments can we either do what we will or claim to love Jesus.

———

It is the Christian paradox that we free ourselves from the burden of the law only when we have accepted the burden of the law.

———

In his poem about being God's prisoner, John Donne expresses a profound truth. Enslaved to Christ, we are, though sinners, de-slaved to sin.

———

Over the doors of the courthouse in Worcester, Massachusetts, is inscribed the line *Obedience to law is the greatest liberty*. Whether this is from Socrates, Aristotle, George Washington or Will Rogers, the statement is worthy of St. Paul.

———

Where a law is restrictive without being liberative it is an imposition. It is the work of an imposter and is lacking in the first purpose of law.

———

To say "It is only a man-made law" is to miss the point. Only when civil laws are at variance with the laws of God are they strictly man-made.

Like every good short of God himself, law can become an end in itself. It can become more than the love it is meant to serve.

———

In the religious life it is possible to keep rules for the love of rules and not for the love of God.

———

To choose which of God's laws to obey is to obey none of God's laws. If some are rejected no merit goes to those which are accepted. A man may die from one bullet or a hundred; he is still dead.

———

Jesus lived under obedience "even unto death," yet he was more free than anyone before or since.

———

Take away law and you have no terms of reference or standards of comparison. You are on your own, and nothing is more lonely and less free than that.

———

The laws of nature are there to emphasize the necessity of the laws of God. From a knowledge of material things, St. Paul reminds us, we come to acknowledge the existence of spiritual things. We are "inexcusable", he says, if we do not follow the argument from nature to God.

———

Natural laws are either interesting or beautiful or mysterious or accounting for everything according to the way we look at them. They are designed to illumine the law of God. They are even designed to reveal the mind of God.

———

Looked at in the wrong way, nature can be a substitute for God. This is because relative beauty can be jealous of absolute beauty.

———

Looked at pictorially, scientifically, romantically or for what can be got out of it to satisfy a greed, nature which is meant to be a stepping-stone towards God becomes a stumbling-block to the knowledge and love of God.

———

Because love gives and receives in human terms there must be order in the giving and receiving. God blesses the exchange but he must also be allowed to govern it. To evade his authority is to sacrifice liberty in giving and receiving.

EXTERIOR AND INTERIOR PEACE

Some people, like Ares the Thracian, delight in battle for its own sake. They enjoy neither external nor internal peace. The first because even when it comes to them they do not prize it, the second because without knowing it they are greedy for what they have not got.

———

People who look for trouble find it. But the bitter-sweet satisfaction it affords them is not worth the trouble of looking for it.

———

People who look too eagerly for peace too often do not find it. This is partly because they do not know where to look, and partly because when it is given to them they do not recognize it for what it is.

———

A man who senses another's peace and is envious of it is likely to miss the peace which is meant for him and which he has only to stretch out his hand to grasp.

———

Like happiness and getting on with people, peace is not always something which we appreciate at the time. When it is withdrawn we know what we have lost, and then feel cheated.

———

Neither exterior nor interior peace can be secured by sitting in a nutshell and not thinking. "I do not want the peace of a stone" Ghandi is reputed to have said.

In order to attain to peace, whether exterior or interior, we have to make the effort – even fight for it by eliminating its opposites. It is nevertheless a gift and not something to be obtained by brute force.

———

We can make a fetish of peace, denying the calls of charity in trying to safeguard it. "Holiness before peace" said Newman, who was never left in peace, outward peace, for long.

———

Peace is a fair enough index of love and prayer, but both love and prayer can exist without it.

———

Though he tells us to "seek after peace and pursue it" the psalmist is careful not to say that we deserve it. It is the most elusive quarry in the world.

———

Who can prove that a flower or a sunset is beautiful? These things can be compared but not proved. Nor can you prove peace. All you can do is to compare exterior with interior peace, peace between nations with peace between individuals, your own peace in one place with your own peace in another.

———

As you cannot see the wind and can see only its effects, so you cannot see peace but only its effects. The moment you try to pin it down you lose it. And probably you lose its effects also.

In promising peace to men of goodwill the angels spoke the language of spiritual orthodoxy. What matters is the will. Where men get their wills right with God and their fellow men they are able to receive the grace of peace from God.

When our Lord speaks about the world's peace and his peace being quite different, what are the essential terms of comparison? At best the world offers order, security, leisure, absence of strife. Jesus offers a state of mind which can exist, and be maintained, where these elements not only are lacking but are in no possible likelihood of being realized.

Though peace has to be earned like everything else it never seems quite what we were working for. Perhaps we worked for it too earnestly and made the mistake of thinking we deserved it.

At those rare times when we are at peace within and without we are so afraid of losing it that already it is slipping away.

Thinking about interior peace destroys interior peace. The patient who constantly feels his pulse is not getting any better.

Restlessness drives a man more urgently than ambition. He longs to get the work over, to reach the end of the day, to look for tomorrow's solace. The next thing, the next thing, the next thing . . . and none of them satisfies.

Apart from inordinate desire and deliberate infidelity, the greatest obstacle to interior peace is the inability to settle. To be homeless is worse for peace than to be homesick.

———

To be at peace a man must have roots and feel he belongs. If he cannot settle in a place, in a job, in a social environment, he does not give himself a chance. But it is not always his fault that a man is a loner and a drifter. It is not always his fault that a man cannot find peace. It is certainly his misfortune.

———

Even peace in failure is not so difficult to maintain as peace when in a state of nervous tension. The interior life involves an element of tension but it is not meant to induce scruples, obsessive fears, psychotic disorders.

———

A soul divided against itself can never find peace. Peace cannot exist where there are contrary loyalties. For true peace there has to be psychological and moral harmony. Conscience must be at rest.

———

I can talk about peace till I am blue in the face. I can search for it until I despair and give up in disgust. I can resign myself to having to do without it for the rest of my life. Why do I not put my case to the Prince of Peace and ask for a share of his peace?

STILLNESS, STABILITY, SILENCE

"The charm of solitude, quiet, silence" Andrey Sinyavsky writes, "is that you can hear your soul speak." So much for the charm of these things, but the value lies in being able to hear *God* speak.

———

The conversation between your soul and God never stops, but you do not give yourself time to listen to it and draw conclusions from it. You need to do more than speak. You need to establish a stillness in which to speak. And hear.

———

When you have hollowed out an enclave of stillness inside your soul you do not have to worry about how to speak and what to say. God draws the response from you that he wants.

———

Just as external and internal conditions combine to create the state of peace, so external and internal conditions create the disposition necessary for contemplation.

———

You cannot pray when the atmosphere vibrates with tension, anxiety, noise, speed, fuss. If you are to pray you must wait until the outward simmers down and the inward is quiet enough to think. Contemplation does not come easily in an airport terminal.

———

People imagine they cannot quiet their mental disturbances enough to pray. They are wrong. There may be an underlying distress, but there is no reason why it should be allowed to become an overlaying distress.

———

Human situations are never so overpowering as to rule out prayer. Prayer directs the human situation, the human relationship, the human sorrow. Prayer may be influenced by these things but not overpowered by them. Not even directed by them.

———

Do I want to pray or only to think about my human problems? Do I want to pray or simply to kneel there contemplating my sorrow? Do I want to direct my prayer towards God or let it direct itself towards me?

———

People imagine they cannot pray or find the quiet they need for prayer if they go on living where they are. So they move from place to place. Do they ever find the quiet they want? And if they do, does it bring them peace? It more likely makes them lonely. God is the best judge of how much quiet we need.

———

Problems connected with recollection and silence will persist throughout life but they are better met by stability than by experiment in locality.

———

If I cannot find rest externally or internally where I am, and if I run to an oasis in the desert, and if I pitch my tent as far from my fellow nomads as possible, and if I then question myself with absolute honesty, what answer shall I give on these two points: Have I run from the grace of acceptance to what may turn out to be a mirage? Am I not a little lonely and bored?

———

Contemplation does not go with running about and being a periodic dropout. Unsteady people, whatever their virtues in other directions, are seldom very prayerful.

———

The unstable man wanders about the world looking for himself. He does not know who he is or where he is meant to be. He lives from one guess to another. His one desire is to get away.

———

"The greatest revelation is stillness." At first sight this, from Lao-Tse, seems nonsense. God is the greatest revelation. Perhaps what is meant is that it is only in stillness that God reveals himself.

———

Stillness is not the negation of disquiet. It plays a positive role. It points, it reveals, it teaches.

———

Once the blessedness of stillness is understood for what it is, we see how it can become, like the scriptures, at once a revelation and a therapy. In its quiet is echoed the healing word of God.

———

As stillness and silence are not the absence of noise, so peace is something more than the absence of conflict. All three suppose a presence, even an activity. They will reign after noise and conflict are over.

———

Before most of God's major works, and acting as an introduction, there was stillness. In the void before creation, in the womb before the nativity, in the tomb before the resurrection. Will it be there before the last trumpet sounds?

———

When do you feel at peace? You will find that the setting is stillness. But perhaps you will notice this only on looking back.

———

There must be times when a man may feel his senses, exterior and interior, to be at rest. He is watching the sun rise over the mountain; he is seeing the colors change in the sky; he feels the morning air fresh on his face. If he hears the rustle of leaves it does not break the silence but deepens it. But this is a foretaste of peace; it does not satisfy. But it is something that it points to everlasting peace.

PENITENCE AND AMENDMENT

It can take less than a minute to commit a sin. It takes not as long to obtain God's forgiveness. Penitence and amendment should take a lifetime.

———

Penitence is not something which can be left behind when amendment is promised. The test of amendment is the continuance of penitence.

———

Penitence does not consist in a list of penitential exercises. It is a disposition of the heart and mind and will. Penitential exercises may or may not be required by God. Penitence is certainly required by God.

———

It is not only sinners who are expected to be penitent. If it were an attitude suited to the guilty alone, why would the most innocent of saints be so often noted for their penitence?

———

There are theologians who tell us that Jesus, being sinless, cannot be called a penitent. But in "becoming sin" for us and "bearing our iniquity" he must surely have taken on man's debt of penitence. Theologians notwithstanding, Jesus did penance for us, instead of us, and as an example to us.

———

"His name is holy who dwells in the high and holy place" Isaias says, "and with a contrite and humble spirit; to revive the spirit of the humble and to revive the heart of the contrite." God does not have to amend, but he does want to show us the necessity for amendment, for humility, for contrition.

——————

Remorse is not necessarily penitence. A man whose desire is to escape the sense of shame may be full of remorse but he is not full of penitence.

——————

An apostate who recants and comes back is like the beautiful prince in the fairy tale who is turned into a toad for his misdeeds and who, after being a good toad, is finally restored to his human state. He is now a more beautiful prince than he was before.

——————

"Man's great guilt does not lie in the sins that he commits" wrote Martin Buber, "but in the fact that he can turn away from evil at any moment and yet does not." Pardon is forever hovering, waiting to be invited.

——————

Sin is something inside our fallen selves trying to come out and be free to hurt. The evil outside ourselves in the fallen world is something which is trying to come in — also to hurt.

——————

The presence of evil is not like the presence of God which is everywhere. Evil is contained, is never wholly free. Though it is a reality, evil is a potential influence. God is absolute being, so his presence knows no limit.

If evil were abolished tomorrow, being would still exist. If the presence of God were withdrawn from creation tomorrow, creation would no longer exist. The most comforting truth about the universe is that good must finally triumph over evil.

———

However evil I feel the world to be I have always Jesus' affirmation of the Father's love for it. The Father so loves the world as to apply the infinite merit of Christ's passion to its redemption.

———

However evil I feel myself to be I have the infallible conviction that God so loves me as to apply the infinite merit of Christ's suffering to my redemption. He not only saves me from the sentence I deserve but wants my presence with him for all eternity. Nothing but love could express itself in this way.

———

The one absolutely certain fact to which my mind can give absolutely certain consent — and this at any moment of my life — is that God loves me. Following from this is the fact that I can love him back.

———

My sins, my fallen nature, the presence of evil all about me and within me; none of these things is proof against God's love. Singly and collectively God has taken them into account. Love is stronger than sin, hate, death. In God, love does not alter. Not a particle of godlessness can get by.

———

Even in the ocean of evil there are islands of holiness. Islands of truth and beauty. The islands are washed at their shores by evil but are never submerged. At the end the islands will remain and the seas recede. All will be holy ground, and the oceans will be dried up and forgotten.

——————

With so much in the world calling out for pardon the incentive to penitence should be compelling. But is it? How often am I moved by it?

——————

When sacrifices are everywhere made for indifferent causes, even for unworthy and sinful ones, the call to sacrifice for the love of God should move me to respond. But does it?

——————

It is when the blood of sacrifice is spilled on the wrong altar that God is most reviled. All the more reason then for sacrifice to be offered in the name of truth and on the altar of love.

——————

The world may be in darkness but this should not upset us. Christ is the light of the world. If we bring this truth into the context of our own experience we must know that light inaccessible has invited us to enter into this light. He has asked us not merely to reflect it but to *be* it. Otherwise his words "you are the light of the world, the city seated on a hill, the salt of the earth" are no more than an oratorical flourish. Jesus did not go in for oratorical flourishes.

——————

Entering into his light and living by it, we cannot but bring light to the world. "In thy light we shall see light."

Light encompasses a man's whole being, and if in a spirit of penitence, amendment, and trust we accept this light and try to walk by its implication we are already within the shadowless range of light eternal.

CONFIDENCE AND PESSIMISM

Pessimism is not despondency. Despondency is a mood, pessimism is a habit. Both can be indulged, both corrected. The grace is there; so is the choice.

Good reason can always be found for both pessimism and despondency. The state of the world, the unfairness of life, personal failure. But there are better reasons for living in a state of confidence.

Confidence is neither facile optimism nor effervescent euphoria. Confidence is a matter of the will; the will to take God's promises seriously.

Frequently people are puzzled that in the gospels there is no mention of Jesus smiling. But there is no mention of Jesus writing (except what he traced in the sand in front of the elders) or referring to created beauty (unless his reference to the temple buildings can be taken as such). Cannot his smiling be equally taken for granted?

That Jesus never smiled is not to be thought of. To anyone with full confidence in the Father, smiling must come naturally.

It is only the inhibited who cannot smile. Inhibition is fear, and fear eats away at confidence, and without confidence there is pessimism. Beyond a certain point pessimism becomes despair.

No saint can be a pessimist. Not only does the saint have hope in regard to himself but also in regard to the human race. No single person is to the saint a hopeless case.

The nearer the saint approaches to the innocence of Christ the nearer he approaches to the innocence of his own childhood. On both counts confidence is the appropriate expression.

A child who is a pessimist would be abnormal. In putting children before us as our models, Jesus as good as forbids us to be pessimistic. Yet of how many Christians can it be said that they habitually look for the best, expect the best, are grateful for the best that is given them?

"Do not be sad" Jesus said. And again "I have told you this so that my joy may be yours." Can he have said these things while himself remaining stiff-faced? How can he have convinced the apostles that he meant what he was saying unless he showed them his gladness?

We have as our image Christ enduring his agony in the garden of Gethsemane, but this is not the whole picture. There was Christ at Nazareth as well. Christ on Tabor. Christ at Bethany with Martha, Mary, and Lazarus.

Someone who talks to children, goes to weddings, mixes with feasting publicans, accepts invitations from worldly people, must be someone who shows pleasure and even gaiety. Had our Lord not felt these things, and shown that he felt them, he would not have been truly human.

———

We can so concentrate on the divinity of Christ as to see too little of the human. In the early church Christians were having to decide whether Christ was more man than God or more God than man. We should not have the same difficulty today.

TRUE AND FALSE SUFFERING

Suffering is a grace granted to those whom God judges to be generous enough to give back to him.

———

Patient endurance of suffering is as worth while as perseverance in prayer or the cultivation of solitude, reading, silence, work. But if it is to be truly spiritualized it must be humble as well as patient. The sufferer must not see himself framed in the crown of thorns.

———

The way that people react to suffering gives the clearest indication of their worth. While everyone would admit this as a truism not everyone draws the practical conclusion.

———

The sufferings of truly good people are made worse by the feeling that they are suffering badly and to no purpose. This, in the providence of God, is the major part of the suffering and the reason for it.

———

Those who most deplore their lack of courage and resignation are often those who are most called upon to suffer. Their sense of inadequacy in suffering is more painful to them than the suffering itself.

———

To be aware while suffering that here is the test, that the supreme choice must now be made, that Christ's cross is being offered for acceptance or rejection creates in the humble soul a scorching sense of dread. What is dreaded is not the suffering but the knowledge of not being up to it.

The prospect of physical pain cannot but cause physical shrinking. It must have done this to our Lord and the martyrs. The prospect of spiritual pain, since there is no knowing what form it is likely to take, causes no more than a vague disquiet. Yet when it comes, spiritual pain is the harder to bear.

Physical pain can be localized. Spiritual pain seems to know no boundaries. With physical pain you can put your finger on where it hurts. Spiritual pain pervades the whole being.

Even where it cannot be reduced by medical means, physical pain can be met and calculations made. The whole point of spiritual trials is that the sufferer does not know where they come from or how to meet them.

Suffering and prayer are alike in this since inevitably each brings its sense of failure to respond to opportunity. If the mistake in the case of prayer is to allow discouragement, in the case of suffering it is to allow self-pity.

We are so often told that we need more faith that mere familiarity weakens the statement. Faith is, nevertheless, the solution.

True suffering, false suffering. True prayer, false prayer. True service, false service. Let us be through with this and live the life God gives us as best we can.

THE GIFT OF TIME

Time may be invisible but it is a material good on a level with such things as possessions, health, success.

It is not only to escape boredom that we escape into time-spending activities; it is to escape life.

When its value is suddenly discovered, time which has been wasted has to be bought back. The cost is higher than that of the activity which wasted it.

The terms used in connection with time are significant: "my own time," "killing time," "filling in time," "I haven't got time." They show how little we think of time as being a gift from God.

At one extreme time can be cheerfully thrown away, at the other it can become an obsession. Indolence is the cause and effect of the former, scrupulosity is the cause and effect of the latter.

Where time has become an obsession there can be no true rest. Prayer is invaded by the worry of what to do next. A certain mental spaciousness is necessary for prayer. Preoccupation with time disallows this.

Where the body is rushing to save time, the mind is too busy to think of God in simplicity. There is not only the fear that we may be wasting precious time but there is also the fear that others may be waiting to encroach upon it.

———

For steady, quiet, objective, simple prayer we need to come to terms with time. Nothing so makes for nervous tension as the thought that we have only a limited time in which to get in our prayers, our work, our social and charitable duties.

———

In the context of spirituality time must be seen as one of the talents which, if it is not traded with, will be buried under the rubble of useless cares.

———

If time is not to be either hoarded or pressed out of existence it must be spent as possessions are spent; not solely for personal use but for others.

———

Ideally speaking time given to others is time given to God. Ideally speaking it is only when time is stolen from God – that is to say from prayer, the need of others and from the duties of our state – that it is wasted. But we need the light of grace to see this and act on it.

———

From the day when Jesus was found by his parents in the temple and the day when he changed the water into wine at Cana we know nothing about how the most important people in the whole history of man spent their time. About fifteen years unaccounted for. Lacking information we can only guess. On one point we do not even have to guess; we know that their time, whatever they happened to be doing, was spent in God.

YOUTH AND MATURITY

They would not admit it but most people want to be counted upon for service of one kind or another. If the old avoid the society of others it is because they can no longer serve.

———

It is more important for the old to maintain serenity and self-respect than to recapture enthusiasm and emotion. Plato held that "if a man is moderate and tolerant, then age need be no burden to him; and if he is not then even youth is full of cares."

———

It is not true that young people know nothing of life. They experience a greater variety of living than the old, feel things more keenly, advance faster. What they do not know is the way life works, its structure, its hazards, its tendency to escape human control.

———

What the adolescent finds bewildering is the struggle of opposite forces within himself, both of which he feels to be part of his nature. The mature person has experienced this struggle so often that he has got used to it. It is not that in maturity we are less concerned but that we are less surprised.

———

The young are puzzled when told to propose to themselves ideals which are not justified by what they see of adult practice. However noble the aspiration urged, and the securities vouched for, the impressionable mind will not be moulded by promises alone.

The disillusion of the young, often brought about by the mindlessness of their elders, is only one degree less harmful than their deliberate corruption.

———

Apart from the direct action of God's grace the most educative force in the process of growing up is the connection, seen and taken to heart, between the ideals and performance of those who are older. Fidelity to the pattern proposed is instinctively recognized as an excellence unequalled in the human makeup.

———

The elderly do not as a rule claim to have been more virtuous than the contemporary young. More often they claim to have been happier. But how can anyone, old or young, measure the happiness of another person – let alone of another generation?

———

The old look back and see that when young they were not as tired as they are now, not as uncomfortable, not as neglected, not as victimized as they are now. What they forget is that if these drawbacks to old age were removed tomorrow they would be no different from what they now are. What they are really complaining about is the loss of youth and not just the advantages of youth.

———

As one gets older one's tranquillity increases but one's expectations decrease. Acceptance is more important than looking forward, but there is less comfort in it.

———

It is generally believed that the nearer an old man draws towards death the more he clings to life. This is not so. He clings to his favorite food and his favorite program on television.

———

Before the age of about forty, people look for a formula which will solve their psychological, moral, and spiritual yearnings. After the age of about forty they settle for peace and a quiet life.

———

Science, philosophy, theology, literature, art, education: all are in the quest for truth. In the last analysis it is not a matter of culture but of religion. It is a matter of rightly ordered spirituality. Why is this not more frankly put to the young?

———

What the young do not realize is that if everything were settled, everything would be dead. Their elders do not realize it either but they are so busy trying to settle things that they have no time to dwell upon such matters.

———

Reaching maturity is painful chiefly because so many conclusions have to be reappraised – if not altogether scrapped. Not that in maturity one is ever quite sure of one's conclusions, but at least one does not have to be forever changing them.

———

When in adult life a man finds he has let go of an ideal which has inspired him in youth, he has to start looking for it again. If he does not he will never, paradoxically, grow up. His maturity will now depend upon his being able to restore the vision – the vision which, again paradoxically, was sacrificed to maturity.

Along with the convictions of faith goes the certainty that one is understood by God. Understood because loved. To be understood is one of the greatest satisfactions we can experience. Not to be understood is one of life's greatest trials.

———

The very young and the very old are handicapped in the matter of understanding. Both classes feel that they cannot enter into minds of those who belong to a generation other than their own. The young man and the old man are at one in this: each feels that others do not know what he is talking about.

———

There is only the thinnest division between what is reasonable and what is rationalized. It is the fault of the grown man and woman to rationalize what is urged by their desires. It is the fault of the adolescent to belittle the reasonable.

———

It is stupid of the young to want to be thought grown up, but it is far more stupid of the old to want to be thought young. It is stupid of the timid to want to be thought brave, but it is far more stupid of those who do not know the meaning of fear to say that at heart they are really cowards. It is natural for fools to want to be thought clever, because if they did not they would not be fools.

PRAYER AND CHARITY

Love of God and love of neighbor are like panels of a looking glass. Set at different angles they show different aspects of the same thing. If we look from one side to the other we do not see in unity.

——————

In an age which endlessly divides and subdivides, we have to guard against missing love's essential unity. We separate the concept of love in contemplation from that of love in activity, love as giving from love as receiving, love in the will from love in the emotions. But when seen in the context of love itself, love is thought of simply as love.

——————

The knowledge of true love is a possession. The communication of true love is a gift. But to talk too much about either is a mistake.

——————

If perfect love is embodied in Christ, then our effort to reflect perfect love will inevitably contain elements of suffering, rejection, apparent failure.

——————

It is comforting to reflect that before the judgment seat of God, love will be the one credential which satisfies. It will be the final exonerating test. Will other things have meant so much to me in this life that I shall be found wanting in the one thing necessary when it comes to the assessment in the next?

Even if I have nothing to show for my time on earth but my desire to love I shall have qualified, I shall have passed from death to life. To have passed from one extreme to another can be attributed to one thing only. Love takes me from darkness to light. Everything that I have done will be shed but love will survive. My infidelities will be blotted out when I come before the face of the merciful God. My mistakes forgotten, my sorrows turned into joy. Only the movement of love will continue, eternally returning to the source of love itself.

———

God has pledged himself to put aside man's sins, his inconsistencies, his stupidity. So long as love is my purpose my salvation is already on the way. But let it be really love and not the desire to be thought loving.

———

The life of Christ is not simply a thing written. It is a thing lived. My sanctification lies in re-living this life in the context of my own life. It lies in identifying myself with the mind of Christ which is primarily the mind of love.

———

If charity were less important, the deviations from charity would not only be less serious but would also be less liable to call themselves by any name except the honest one of sin. All virtue is loving right, all sin is loving wrong.

———

The world has a great deal to say about love. So also has the gospel. Where the world rejects the face of love as presented by the gospel it ends up with a caricature. There is just enough likeness in the false picture to see where the original came from but not enough to justify the travesty into which it is turned.

The right ordering of love, which means the fusion of charity towards God and man, inevitably brings about the right ordering of prayer. Not only will the purity of a man's prayer be proportionate to the purity of his love, but the value of his prayer to the general good will be measured by the quality of his love.

———

A man who prays incessantly is one who loves incessantly. He could not do it otherwise. The sad thing is that this joint movement towards God and man can be slowed down, and even halted, by selfishness, laziness, greed.

———

In order to serve God it is not enough to hound down the enemies of love. What is more important is to purify the promptings of love. The light of grace is needed here because when we talk about the pure intention of our love, especially in the case of human love, we are apt to talk a lot of hypocritical nonsense.

———

Self-deceptions flourish more luxuriantly in the field of love than anywhere else. What is claimed to be altruistic love can, under frank observation, reveal itself to be nothing more noble than sensual desire. People are less honest about love than they are about money, and this is saying a good deal.

———

Hecaton of Rhodes has this to say about the exchange of affection: "I will show you a love potion which is without herbs, physic, or witches' brew. If you want to be loved, then love."

While the possible pitfalls of human love are revealed to us by prayer, it is about its possible blessings that prayer has even more to teach.

———

The only true sacrifice is that which has its inspiration and end in charity. Sacrifice is the appropriate expression of both charity and prayer.

———

The only value which Christianity sees in voluntary renunciation is that which relates it to love. True renunciation renounces that which is opposed to love, and enhances that which leads to it.

———

What makes our lives worth while is stretching towards God who is love and truth. That we reach out beyond our capacity is at once our pain, our adventure, our hope.

———

It is one thing to think in a Christian way on the race issue; it is another to show in Christian practice how opposed to Christ's love is discrimination.

———

Love prevents faith from being rationalized; faith prevents love from being secularized; hope prevents faith and love from looking for reward in this life only.

———

The constructive, according to the Swami Sivananda Sarasvati, will always defeat the destructive. "Courage triumphs over fear, patience over anger, generosity over avarice, compassion over hatred and indifference." We Christians, with our faith, hope, and charity, should be able to bear this out.

HYPOCRISY AND TRUTH

The first meaning of hypocrisy is the use of virtue as a cover in order to deceive others as to one's actions or character. A deeper meaning is lying to oneself and forcing belief in the lie.

Hypocrisy is not only falsifying humility but falsifying truth. It is bad to offend against either, but of the two it is worse to offend against truth.

Jesus is the pattern of humility but he is the essence of truth. We are called to imitate his humility but to bear witness to his truth.

Essentially it is not the discrepancy between principle and practice which makes the hypocrite, but the refusal to acknowledge the discrepancy.

A hypocrite is not someone who fails to live up to the principles he proclaims but someone who pretends to be living up to them when he knows he has ceased to try.

Since you cannot either tell or live a lie without knowing it, an unconscious hypocrite is a contradiction in terms.

A man may be a drunkard, a cheat, an adulterer without being a hypocrite. It is canonizing his vices and taking care that others see only his virtues that make a man a hypocrite.

The man who does not condone his weaknesses but deplores them, who does not look for the recognition of his virtues but prefers them to be forgotten, who is not interested in getting himself a good reputation whether or not he deserves it, is unlikely to turn into a hypocrite. But have you ever met such a man?

———

What we want others to think we are like is no indication of what we are really like. All it shows is our weakness in not being able to justify the impression.

———

By playing our cards with skill we can cause people to have the highest opinion of us. But what sort of person is it who exists only in the minds of other people?

———

We may call ostentation, ambition, sentimentality, stubbornness and indolence by nicer names but we cannot disguise the effects these qualities produce. Effects are not so easily rationalized.

———

Even if we can give convincing excuses for our behavior we seldom think we deserve the consequences of our behavior.

———

A failure which can be put down to nerves, exhaustion, or inability to face the inevitable need not necessarily be sinful. The weakness lies in a lack of trust. There is little difference between this and lacking the will to resist temptation.

Nowhere does self-deception flourish more harmfully than in the spiritual life. When worldly people delude themselves about their intelligence, ability, and appearance it does not matter so much, but when religious people persuade themselves that they are serving God when in fact they are serving self it matters a good deal.

——————

Once a person has seriously taken on the practice of prayer he does not have to hide any more. Whatever the psychological flaws in his character – at one extreme pushing him into self-sufficiency and at the other paralysing him with self-hatred – he finds in prayer the answer to his problem. He can rely on God where before he was hypnotized by self.

——————

It would be wrong to cling to a course of action for no better reason than that it has been resolved upon. The motives for perseverance have to be constantly re-examined and held up to the light of God's love.

——————

The sterile soul, untouchable in its so-called fidelity, is not merely opting out and remaining neutral; the offence is positive and assertive of self.

——————

The only corrective to rigidity on the one hand and libertarianism on the other is honesty. Honesty with God, with others, and with oneself. The worst form dishonesty can take is hypocrisy.

——————

If to be a hypocrite is to assume a false identity, then honesty means shedding the disguises which either we have acquired by our own ingenuity or else allowed ourselves to be vested with by others. It also means admitting that the disguises were no good.

TEMPTATION AND SIN

We know, when not immediately tempted, that Christ endured every temptation experienced by man. But in the heat of passion, even allowing the presence of mind to remember it, this fact seems impossible to believe and so is no help. The powers of evil work day and night to withdraw this help.

You can confidently say that being charitable is more important than being industrious, and that murder is more serious than being spiteful. But you cannot say that one man's sin is worse than another's because you do not know another's mind and will.

Even at the end of a whole chain of self-deceptions a man is as culpable as he knows himself to be.

To compare one man's guilt with another's – or even, on outward evidence alone, your own at different periods of your life – is as foolish as to compare a child's conscience with an adult's.

With our own minds so full of flaws as we know them to be it should be easy not to condemn others whose minds are also full of flaws. Even if we have managed not to condemn, we still find it almost impossible not to judge.

Christ tells us not to judge if we want to escape judgement ourselves. He further tells us to be merciful if we want to receive mercy. Showing mercy to others means more than extending a vague and noncommittal forgiveness.

———

Pity is sympathy for another in his problem or his sickness or his poverty or his bereavement. It is a good thing to give but an embarrassing one to receive. Mercy and compassion are another matter.

———

Where the thrust of pity is outward, the thrust of compassion is inward. Identifying with another's sorrow, entering into another's mind with understanding, and so far as possible sharing the emotion: this is compassion.

———

In order to feel for others in their temptations and sins we do not have to have experienced their temptations and sins. We are not expected to share their guilt but we are expected to understand their guilt. For every act of charity towards others, understanding is the primary condition.

———

That Jesus fought despair and triumphed we know from his prayers on the cross which began with "My God, why have you forsaken me?" and ended with "Into your hand, Lord, I commend my spirit." However near we come to despair, we have this precedent to refer to.

———

Because they relate to God directly, the theological virtues are most subject to attack. When we feel we have no faith, hope, or love we feel we have reached the end of the line. If we were to give in here we would have.

SUFFERING AND DETACHMENT

"I believe that humanity has but one objective" wrote Flaubert in his diary, "namely to suffer." Flaubert would be thought very old-fashioned today. In the spirituality of the future there may be much reliance on communication and fellowship, but unless there is a corresponding reliance on the mystery of suffering where will be Christ's sacrifice? Will men and women have enough to draw upon in their sufferings?

If for Christians the whole of religion is summed up in a particular person, then that particular person must be seen as engaged in his most significant work. Those who accuse the Christian tradition of making too much of suffering are accusing it of making too much of Christ.

"For this cause came I unto this hour" our Lord said. What hour was that? Not the hour of acclamation when the crowds wanted to crown him king. Not the hour of popular demonstration on Palm Sunday. Not even the hour of transfiguration when the Father bore witness to his divinity or the hour of his baptism when the Holy Spirit rested upon him and proclaimed his membership in the Blessed Trinity. The hour awaited was the hour of his rejection, the hour of failure, of loneliness, of pain and of shame.

It is significant that Jesus did not say "If any man will be my disciple let him take up his comforts and follow me." The word was "cross." Not "joy," not "pleasure," not even "peace," but "Let him take up his cross," were the words he used.

———

If we can accept our sufferings and unite them with his, we shall have no difficulty in uniting our joys with his.

———

It is a curious fact that since pre-Christian times the cup has been the symbol of two elements in human life which run contrary to one another: pleasure and pain. In the Christian dispensation this should not surprise us. What we think of as the chalice of salvation must contain vinegar as well as wine.

———

For many of us the greatest cross is the fear of having to bear the cross. It means we have forgotten Christ's promise about the burden being light when borne with him and the yoke being sweet by those who submit for his sake to its bitterness.

———

Anxiety about what may never happen may be idle, may be something not to be indulged in, may be unworthy – but it is a real suffering, and as such finds a place in Christ's passion.

———

When mortification is identified with fanaticism, and the cross with medieval superstition, there will have to be a lot more charity in the church to make good what is likely to be lost.

The Christian is never more wholly a Christian, more wholly a servant of his fellow Christians, more wholly himself than when suffering for the love of God. The church is never more wholly itself, more wholly apostolic, more wholly in the tradition of sanctity than when persecuted and producing martyrs.

The church's glory is not its power and numerical superiority, nor its system or its discipline or its theology. Its glory lies in its willingness to sacrifice.

Detachment, which is the purpose of mortification, is not something either piecemeal or transient. Answering the call to detachment is like launching a boat: you cannot launch bits of it. Perseverance in detachment means hauling up the gangplank and burning it.

If Jesus' whole teaching rests on love, then acceptance of that teaching must involve suffering. He who was all love ended his life in suffering. The connection between love, truth, and suffering is not accidental but essential and logical.

Lights in prayer are meant to come and go. We see by them for a moment and then the darkness closes in again. We may not hoard the lights or we may lose the grace of darkness.

Fireflies stop glowing when we catch them and put them in a jam pot and expect them to serve as a lantern. Better to walk in the dark and let the fireflies do their job.

ADAPTATION AND COMPROMISE

Adaptation is bowing to obedience and to sheer moral and physical necessity. Compromise is giving in to pressures which are dubious, retrograde, and more of the world than of God.

———

There is all the difference between legitimate adaptation and convenient compromise. The difference is not easy to see when good people urge compromise in the name of legitimate adaptation.

———

It is only imperative to change when the imperatives are spiritual and moral. Even then it has to be proved that the imperatives are really so.

———

Considerations of majority opinion, reasonable excuse, social or financial advantage — all of which are worldly options — do not justify adaptation, still less compromise.

———

Before you change an accepted order, tradition, or observance you need to assure yourself on three points: that you know the intention of whoever was originally responsible; that the purpose is no longer served; that what you want to replace it with is intrinsically better.

Few texts from scripture are so misread as "all things to all men." The words are for self-examination, not for self-justification.

———

The good of keeping an open mind is nullified if it means swerving from a course decided upon in prayer to be right. Flexibility in responding to the immediate grace is a good; flexibility in responding to the prevailing trend is bad.

———

Few convictions have a built-in security of their own. If they had there would be no need for faith.

———

Acquiescense is more often spinelessness than the acknowledgment of another's valid claims, more often turning a blind eye than looking the thing in the face and being genuinely forced to agree.

———

To please on every occasion is not the first aim of the Christian. There are occasions when the Christian has to do the opposite. If our Lord had set himself always to please he would not have attacked the Pharisees, shocked his host and fellow guests by taking a harlot's part at a dinner, thrown out the money-changers from the temple and so offended the priests.

———

The rich young man drew back from full discipleship because he knew he would want to make compromises. The three would-be followers drew back because they could not take on the vocation without making qualifications. Jesus was uncompromising: "Once the hand is laid on the plough, no one who looks back is fit for the kingdom of heaven."

———

To water down orthodoxy to make it acceptable is not to help in spreading the faith. It is to bypass the faith. It is to belittle one of the few things in life which may not be belittled.

SENSE AND SPIRIT

As his letters to the Romans and Corinthians show, for St. Paul the essential classification of mankind was not into the sinful and the innocent, the pagan and the faithful, the enslaved and the free. The difference was between the sensual and the spiritual. The man of sense rejects the life of faith. The spiritual man accepts what the Spirit teaches. The one backs his refusal by indulging his desires; the other backs his recognition by denying them.

——————

The sensual man is at home in worldliness because he has no higher aspiration. The spiritual man, however much attracted to worldliness, cannot be at home in the world of sense because he is groping towards the world of spirit.

——————

The sensual man claims independence of faith, of law, of service. The spiritual man submits to all three and finds his independence in so doing.

——————

The fact that a man is a Christian does not place him in the category of the spiritual. Nor is the man who is not a Christian put among the carnal. It depends upon what each one chooses as a way of life to follow.

——————

Sensual gratification is not the sole qualifying factor which distinguishes the carnal man. An interest in prayer is not the sole qualifying factor in the case of the spiritual.

Secular conformism, presentation of a false image, ambition at the expense of others, emphasis on money and position: these are the marks of "living in the flesh." Leaving the disposal of life to God, referring decisions to gospel principles, trying to reflect Christ's life: these are the marks of "living in the spirit."

———

I would rather be a pagan who lives up to the light God gives him than a Christian who denies such light. "He that is not with me is against me" our Lord said. His doctrine here was explicit: those who claimed to see the difference between sin and innocence were more guilty in their transgressions than those who were without this knowledge.

LETTER AND SPIRIT

"The letter kills, the spirit gives life." Few texts are more often made use of to serve a selfish end. It can be quoted to excuse almost any transgression.

———

Only when it is given a higher place than the virtue which it enshrines does the letter kill. St. Paul was comparing the words of the covenant with the meaning of the covenant. He was telling the Corinthians that the meaning was the thing to look for.

———

Without the wording there would be no covenant, no commandments, no gospels and no sacraments. Given the frame of words, we look for the spirit which has been breathed into it.

———

With man's fatal gift of mistaking the priorities the symbol can be substituted for what is symbolized. Thus can the spirit be extinguished.

———

So long as the letter is the servant of the spirit and not its master, the spirit gives life to the letter. Hence public worship. Hence vocal prayer.

———

Too many words can smother prayer. Too few can let it disintegrate. The aim should be to use whatever means God sends at any one time. Words today, silence tomorrow, a mixture of both the day after. In whatsoever state of prayer I am, I am content therewith.

When our Lord told the Samaritan woman that worship of the Father should be in spirit and in truth he was not ruling out considerations of place, ceremonial, formulas. He was saying that these factors were useless unless animated by spirit and truth.

"Our Father who art in heaven." This is letter as well as spirit.

We may propose to ourselves an abstract prayer, a prayer of silence and simple waiting, but if the spirit and truth of our prayer are felt to be escaping us it is time to call in the support of words. The words here do not kill but conserve.

While it is true that worship does not consist in things said but in the intention directed, it is nevertheless difficult to will an intention without formulating it.

Prayer might not present to us such a problem if we were more ready to follow the example of the apostles who asked our Lord to teach them how to pray. We spend so much time educating ourselves in prayer that we forget who it is who alone can teach it.

The boy Samuel was told by Heli to pray: "Speak, Lord, for your servant listens." He was not instructed to say: "Listen, Lord, for your servant speaks." If we listened more we would learn more about spirit and truth . . . and in turn would be better able to worship in spirit and in truth.

———

"The letter kills, the spirit gives life." It is easy enough to see how the wrong sort of letter can kill the spirit. It is not so easy to see how the wrong sort of spirit can kill the letter.

———

If the liturgy without heart and mind co-operating is pointless, heart and mind which scorn a liturgy are presumptuous.

TRUE AND FALSE ZEAL

There is a difference between the man of zeal and the zealot. The man of zeal can afford to be patient. The zealot is aggressive, pressing his reforming measures in a rush and trampling over people's feelings.

——————

Just as personal piety is spoiled by wanting to be thought holy, so the more general desire to make other people pious can be spoiled by wanting to be thought a leader of reform or a director of souls. It is the greatest mistake to want to be thought anything.

——————

True leaders of reform will want to work in the background. They will want to turn all the attention on Christ. They will know that "no other foundation is laid" for reform or conversion or salvation itself "but which is laid, which is Jesus Christ."

——————

Jehu, son of Josaphat, was filled with zeal for the Lord of Hosts. But he was ruthless, going about the work with bitterness in his heart and blood on his hands. In the end he did not achieve much in the way of reform.

——————

True reform must be prompted by love, directed towards love, carried out in love. Otherwise it goes round in circles like a whirlpool, coming back to its center which is itself.

True zeal is the exact opposite to a whirlpool. Its influence goes out like the rings on the surface of a lake when a stone has been dropped into the water. The true reformer here is the stone which is lost to view.

———

The biblical account of Gideon and his fleece can be taken as an illustration of how the reformer's zeal should operate. It should be as the dew which penetrates the existing material. The gentle absorption is likely to be far more effective than the exercise of violence.

———

Elias had to be shown that the spirit of the Lord was not in the whirl-wind and the storm, not in the crashing of rocks or the roll of thunder. It was to be known in the soft whisper of the breeze.

THE GIFT OF FOOLISHNESS

"The foolish has God chosen to confound the wise," St. Paul said, and was ready himself "to become a fool for Christ's sake." If this were not enough to give a blessing to honest stupidity we have our Lord thanking the Father for "hiding these things from the learned and the clever, and revealing them to mere children." Children are more often associated with folly than with wisdom.

Every era has rightly paid homage to true wisdom. In our own era intellectualism does duty for wisdom.

Where words and speculations mask the absence of thought you get nothing wrapped in nothing. The child in the story is often quicker than the bemused adult to see that the emperor is wearing no clothes.

There is no virtue in cleverness as such or in foolishness as such. The clever may be humble and the foolish may be proud. But of the two classes humility favors fools. The clever should be clever enough to refuse the temptation to pride.

Of course we should use the brains God gives us. Of course we should try to be efficient, acquire information, strive after knowledge and experience and wisdom. But all this is limited to our capacity. The horizons of the humble, simple, and uneducated are unlimited.

As champions of the intellect you may cite St. Augustine, St. Thomas, St. Bonaventure, and the many doctors of the church. But think of the many millions who have rubbed along on nothing much more than the direction of the will towards the love of God.

"To live in great simplicity and in a wise ignorance" said St. Pachomius, "is beyond all human wisdom. . . . Most men look for miracles as a sign of holiness, but I prefer a solid humility to raising the dead."

"Unhappy is the man who knows all other things but does not know you, God," said St. Augustine, "and happy is he who knows you though he knows nothing else."

The folly of the saints is more to be envied than their wise perceptions and judgments. Not invariably but often. The influence of sanctity is greatest where holy foolishness and sound judgment balance one another.

It is safer to be mistaken for a fool if you are not one than to be mistaken for a wise man if you are a fool.

In the name of Christian charity we are always being exhorted to suffer fools gladly. It needs just as much Christian charity to suffer clever people gladly.

THE GIFT OF MARRIAGE

Unless marriage is thought of in terms of supernatural vocation even the natural side of it will be incomplete. The material and physical will outweigh the natural and spiritual.

———

To think of marriage as the natural environment for people who do not plan to give their lives to God is to think of it mistakenly on two counts. First it is meant to be a supernatural as well as a natural state; second it is a state which should encourage people to give their lives, and those of their family, to God.

———

For people to think that their physical reactions are responsible for the happiness or unhappiness of their marriage is like thinking that the readings on the barometer are responsible for the weather.

———

To expect two people to live out their lives together in harmony without the help of God is to ask too much of psychology, too much of human character. If God made matrimony, man and woman cannot make matrimony without him.

———

If Christian marriage is to be more than a biological experiment it must be given its spiritual destination. In a secular society Christians have the opportunity of restoring the supernatural to the natural.

Affection, companionship, common interests, mutual respect and enduring devotion: these are the temporal elements in a good marriage. Temporal elements have their eternal dimension.

Suitability helps the security of a marriage, but spirituality, by calling for mutual self-sacrifice, ensures it.

If a man wants to find God everywhere he must find God somewhere. Particularly in his own family.

It is not true that the parents get the children they deserve. Nor is it true that the children get the parents they deserve. It is not a question of *deserving* either affection or estrangement. To every family God gives love freely and abundantly. Each member can co-operate. No member is penalized. There is nothing fatalistic about it or accidental. Family love is there, waiting, and the members can develop it all the time.

Where matrimony is looked upon as a gift from God, as more of his ordering than of man's, everything that flows from matrimony is received with thanksgiving. Children, understanding, confidence, security: these things are seen as having a sacredness about them.

It is a commonplace to claim that a love which is worthy of the name is sacrificial. Each family has its own sacrifices to make for its individual members. But unless the sacrifices demanded are blatantly obvious they are easily taken to be restrictive. Habitually making allowance for the weaker members is the kind of sacrifice which cannot fail.

———

Where the joys of married life are taken as coming from the hand of God, the trials of married life are taken in the same way. Not with resentment but in the terms of the original arrangement: for better or for worse, for richer or for poorer, in sickness or in health.

———

Where members of a family are separated from one another, where poverty or sickness or loss is suffered, the pain is part of the life. Marriages are not made for fun. Families are not kept together for social or economic reasons. The unity of a family is more costly than that of any other group. If this were not so it would not reflect the unity of the holy family.

———

The family of Jesus, Mary, and Joseph was a gift to fallen man. It still is. But because man so seldom sees his own family as reflecting this gift he sees its members more or less superficially and not in depth.

ACCEPTANCE AND FAITH

While accepting in faith the life God sends us we do not have to accept everything that goes with the life God sends us. Apart from the obvious instances of temptation and sin, we still have to fight the evils which surround our lives: injustice, corruption, prejudice, rejection of the truth. Acceptance does not mean sitting still, limp and blindfolded.

———

Am I to assume that the environment in which I find myself is what God has planned for me? May I never resist my environment then, and try to change it for another? The answer depends on how sure you are that your well-being, spiritual and moral and psychological, is being harmed by accepting things as they are.

———

"Father, if it be possible let this chalice pass from me, yet not my will but yours be done." We may pray that the pressure be lifted and the situation altered, but if we are trying to follow Christ we do not take the initiative. We accept the Father's ruling.

———

When we have handed ourselves over to God without qualification, without telling him what he should do with us and how he can get the best out of us, we may end up doing a work for which we feel ourselves unsuited and which seems inconsistent with our original vocation. We may find ourselves separated from the people with whom we most want to be. We shall almost certainly be in a place we dislike. But if we accept all this as being the will of God we shall not lose by it.

To accept the consequences of our surrender to God's wisdom in the handling of our strictly interior search is bound to be harder than resignation to more outward trials. But the rule is the same: humility and trust.

Without having to compromise or condone, without yielding an inch in our ideals, we can come to terms with a spirit which is alien from our own. It is not a question of making concessions to the prevailing culture but of making our peace with life as presented to us within that culture.

We may dislike the age in which we live and may disapprove of its spirit, but it is as useless to resist it as it would be for a fish to resist water or for a bird to resist air.

A man who keeps up a feud with life becomes increasingly self-centered, cynical, obsessed with the unfairness of his lot. His wretchedness is not caused by the circumstances which he resists but by his resistance to circumstances.

Misfortunes in themselves do not defeat a man; it is his attitude towards them that defeat him. There may be nothing he can do under misfortune, but at least he can control its effect upon him.

The man who refuses to co-operate with life, and with God's handling of it, complains wearily of being disillusioned. Finding fault with others and with religion he is unable to contribute anything towards mankind, is unable to find peace, is unable to pray.

The excuse given for disillusion is often the inconsistency of idealists. The charge may be valid enough, but what would happen if there were no idealists? Very soon there would be no ideals.

One of the most difficult things to accept, particularly for the old, is change. Change should be seen not as accidental to life but as part of life itself. Under God, change actually produces life – in the sense of causing the existing order to be what it is. "Everything that exists" wrote Marcus Aurelius, "is the seed of that which will be." Change is not an interruption of the existing order but a reason, humanly speaking, for the present order existing at all.

"He who does not accept the conditions of life" wrote Baudelaire, "sells his soul." Presumably this is because he buys compensations, and having done so, finds the price too high. The most costly thing in the world is escape.

MELANCHOLY AND HOPE

Where melancholy is caused by guilt, the remedy is trust that our repentance has been genuine and God's forgiveness assured.

———

Where melancholy is caused by remembering better days long ago, which is the kind from which the elderly mostly suffer, the best course is not to treat it seriously and never to make comparisons.

———

Where melancholy is caused by temperament, and has proved itself by years of persistence, there is nothing in the world to be done about it. It cannot be cured but can certainly be accepted, not inflicted on others, not wallowed in, and above all offered to God. There can be few better offerings a man can make.

———

To be activated, hope has to work from a willing disposition. There must be the desire to believe in what faith has to say about hope. But this is precisely what, by definition, the melancholy person is unable to do.

———

Few sorrows are more searching than to live at a time and in a society where false principles are generally accepted. But this should not allow one to settle into the habit of melancholy. "That the birds of worry and sadness fly above your head" runs a Chinese proverb, "this you cannot change. But that they build nests in your hair, this you can prevent."

Anything that is found to stimulate hope should be seized upon and made to serve. This applies to a book, a film, a broadcast, or a conversation with someone who can impart it.

Seeing the future as unrelieved gloom for the human race is rarely the melancholic's dominant mental activity. He is more concerned with the wretchedness of his own condition. The here-and-now sadness of living in which there is no likelihood of change. He does not leave room for the action of grace which can alter both the present and the future scene.

The doctrine of the presence of God, to be realized here and now, should give to the habitually unhappy both the light to see what Christian hope is all about and the grace to act upon this light.

It is not that melancholy people lack imagination and are consequently unable to put their trust in the reward held out to them of eternal happiness. They show plenty of imagination in visualizing a past which they think was happier, a number of alternatives to the hideous present, and any amount of horrors which are yet to come. What they lack is the courage to put aside the past, live with God, in the present, and leave the future to divine providence.

Hope and belief in heaven are less of a problem to the worldly and passionate than they are to the cynical. The cynic sneers and feels superior. It is the difference between near-love and near-hate.

———

Our Lord said that unless we became as little children we would not enter the kingdom of heaven. Children have no difficulty about hope or heaven. They may not know much about either but they take both for granted. It is the cynics, because of the pride which makes them look down on these things, who doubt.

———

By letting themselves be cynical, unhappy people aggravate their melancholy. They are like a dog which tears at its wounded paw so as to hurt the pain.

———

To hope for this or that solution to a personal problem, however earnest the prayer, is to tell God how to handle the matter. True hope and true prayer mean trust in God's wisdom and not in self-devised remedies.

———

It is when his desperation stampedes a man into running from what had been his securities that he is in serious danger. But if he has learned to pray properly he will have that particular security left to him. It will tell him that he cannot run forever.

PRAYER

In the vocabulary of the spirit the terms must be understood. Peace is not enjoying tranquillity but being in harmony. Faith is not feeling sure but abiding by conviction. Love is not a warm emotion but the will to praise and serve. Prayer is not a recitation or a ritual or a burning devotion or concentration, but a stretching out to God in praise.

——————

We make the mistake of thinking we must be original in our prayers, sending up to God concepts and aspirations which he had not thought of and which he did not know we could produce. It is God who invents our prayers. It is our privilege that we can listen and respond to his inspiration.

——————

"The word that goes forth from my lips" says the Lord, "must not return to me void." We can echo but we have no words of our own that he has not heard or himself inspired.

——————

God is at once the source and destination of our prayer. His prayer goes back and forth through us. We breathe in his prayer and breathe it out again. The breath of life is his.

——————

When St. Paul tells the Philippians that "it is God who works in you both to will and to accomplish" he is speaking of the whole range of Christian living. But in relation to prayer the doctrine is especially to the point.

God attracts the soul, the soul responds, God crowns the response. God is at once the seeker and the sought. He is at once the singer and the song. He is at once the inspiration and the inspired. He is the beginning and the end, the alpha and omega.

Prayer operates on something more than determination and discipline. Yet without determination and discipline it is not likely to become the abiding reality which it is meant to be. Indeed, it will not survive.

Prayer without discipline and order becomes amorphous, haphazard, a thing to be taken up and dropped according to mood. Prayer without detachment becomes a hobby and an hypocrisy. Prayer is more than a culture, it is an ascesis.

An old and experienced man said: "Until the age of thirty the prevailing temptation is to impurity, from thirty to fifty a man is tempted to worldly ambition, from fifty onwards to defeat and laziness." Since from youth to senility temptation is temptation it is a mistake to make such free pronouncements.

To take up prayer in a spirit of experimentalism is to court discouragement. It will be found not to produce such an aesthetic experience as might have been expected. In the prayer life, as in so much else in life, the subjective is the enemy of the objective. The objective is the greater glory of God.

The best argument which the forces of evil can bring against our prayer is that we are not worthy of the grace of prayer. And the best answer we can make to this is to say that of course we are not.

———

In giving glory to God our prayer bears witness to every good united in the divine simplicity. The less we try to define and departmentalize in our prayer the better for our own simplicity.

———

The presence of evil is alien to our nature, fallen though we are, whereas the presence of God is not. God's presence is the proper element of our existence: the element in which we can be taught to be completely ourselves.

———

We have to consent to the presence of evil before it can engulf us. The presence of God engulfs us anyway. Our prayer consists in making ourselves conscious of this presence and giving the appropriate response.

———

"Whether we are brave or cowardly" wrote Bernanos, "only one thing is important: to be always there where God wants us to be, and for the rest to trust to him." This applies to the whole of life, and particularly to the life of prayer.

———

The senses are none too accurate in their knowledge of the world of sense, so how can they record the yearnings of the spirit? Gaze at the sun and your vision is dazzled so that you cannot see. Yet gazing at God do you expect to be able to see?

——————

In the last analysis the test of prayer lies here: do you want to pray, try to pray, make the decision to go on praying? You can then take your finger off the pulse of your prayer, confident that your search for God in prayer is proof of having found him.

——————

When we think of patience we think of someone with a tired smile putting up with bores. Rather it is putting up with ourselves more than with others. Not because we ourselves are bores – we never think we are – but because we never get any better.

——————

It is true of all life but especially true of the strictly interior life that the humble soul will be the patient soul, and that hanging on patiently gives depths to the soul's humility.

——————

Recognizing our membership of a fallen race, we judge it to be only natural that in the communication of prayer we shall not know where we stand, what to do, how to rise to the fluctuations of darkness and light.

——————

Fallen humanity is like a kite: designed to ride the sky but having crashed on its first flight can never quite be the same again. Though mended and able to take to the air, it is more frail than it was and cannot be sure of flying to the heights proposed.

———

It is in patient prayer — which supposes perseverance as well as dependence — that the soul begins to see how fallen man is. It is one thing to know this academically and another to know it experimentally . . . from the inside.

DARKNESS AND LIGHT

It is a feature of the spiritual life that what is darkness on one plane is light on another, and that what is light on one plane is darkness on the other.

There is darkness which follows deliberate infidelity and there is the darkness which is the action of grace. The former hides God from us, the latter hides us from ourselves.

Where the hedonist does not miss the light because he has never known it, the man of prayer misses it the moment it is withdrawn from him.

The more the man of prayer tries to force the return of the light he once enjoyed, the more he plunges himself in darkness.

If they were only sensible, sinners would renounce their sin and so come into the light, while spiritual people would renounce their investigations and allow God to allot their light and darkness.

We complain of lacking light in prayer, yet when we are granted it we draw the wrong conclusions. We think we have earned it; we take it to be a sign of progress; we believe it to be a greater grace than darkness. On all three points we are mistaken.

To think that we are responsible for the grace which comes to our prayer, whether darkness or light, is as if a glider were to think it had launched itself, as if a television set were to think it had composed the program, as if the blades of a windmill were to think they were revolving by their own effort.

"Let there be light shining out of darkness" God says. From where else – since light shining out of light must lose its force?

"While the night was in the midst of its course" the eternal word was born. Yet we still fear the dark nights of our prayer.

On the authority of St. John of the Cross the element of darkness is safer for prayer than the element of light. Light can too easily lead to overconfidence. Darkness leads to humility and the patient waiting upon God.

Since I am made in the likeness of God I must expect the photograph to be developed in the dark.

As wine matures in the cellar, so prayer matures in the dark.

———

Who should say that the foundations of a house are the least important part? The spiritual life rests on the foundations, on the part which is underground.

———

You are in darkness. Can you still say "The Lord rules me and I shall want for nothing?" Then you are in the grace of darkness. Which means that you are in the light.

———

If our spiritual darkness teaches us nothing more than that we cannot be sure of ourselves, that without the help of grace we are bound hand and foot, that God is our only hope, it has taught us all that we need to know.

———

The dark night of sense passes. The dark night of the spirit passes. The thing which will never pass is the eternal dawn to which these nights are but the fleeting prelude.

TRUE AND FALSE PRAYER

While it may be an overstatement to say that all prayer is true prayer it can nevertheless be said that however misconceived a prayer may be it represents a recognition of grace and a response to it.

——————

Since prayer is the communication between the soul and God there must be on the soul's part an element of truth about it which reflects the truth of God or there would be no response to God at all.

——————

Inscribed on a tombstone in Oxfordshire are the lines:

Here lie I, Martin Elginbrod.
Have mercy on my soul, Lord God:
As I would do if I were God
And thou wert Martin Elginbrod.

——————

"The raising up of the mind and heart to God" is the classical definition of prayer. It contains a number of propositions. "Raising up" – not necessarily being able to keep the prayer thus raised. "Mind and heart" – not necessarily words, imagined scenes, theological speculations. "To God" – as he is, merciful and loving.

——————

For prayer to be spoiled there has to be the deliberate consent to spoil it. Without such consent the prayer, more or less good according to the degree of desire, goes on. No prayer is spoiled accidentally.

———

Those who play about with prayer that is given them are more open to delusion than those who aspire to no more than being able to say the Our Father properly.

———

There have been many near-perfect souls in the history of spirituality who have allowed themselves to be deflected after years of faithful prayer. Where laziness has failed, false mysticism has succeeded.

———

Humility before praying, while praying, after praying, when talking about prayer: this is the safeguard and the disposition without which prayer can never truly get going. It supposes receptivity, trust, resignation. It is the foundation of Mary's prayer.

———

It is pride and not distraction that turns true prayer into false. Once we spend our prayer time congratulating ourselves on our mastery of prayer we should know we have got nowhere in prayer.

———

Only humility can bring false prayer back to the course of truth. Short of a miracle of grace, humble dependence on God is the sole remedy. But then in these circumstances humble dependence on God amounts to a miracle of grace.

RELIGION GENERALLY

Not everyone has a natural love for religion. Most practising Christians accept the obligation of service, take on truth as an abstraction, look upon the church as a necessity. Few like religion as such. But you are not asked to like religion as such.

———

"The just man lives by faith." Faith supposes, since the will is here at issue, the life of love. Taste and natural interest are not the vital concern in the things that relate to God. The vital concern is to will what God wills.

———

Deciding the order of his concerns is the first of man's duties. Next after that comes the attention to be paid to them in terms of everyday conduct.

———

Concerns which are not related to truth – which comprises faith, hope, and charity – are without destination. They may be worthy concerns, humanitarian and ethical concerns, but they do not extend beyond the rim of temporal existence.

———

You do not have to enjoy the consideration of transcendental truths any more than you need to enjoy thinking about existentialism or totalitarianism. You have to accept them on faith. Enjoyment does not enter in.

The church represents Christ, and Christ is truth. Recognize this and you belong to the faith. You may fail as one of the faithful, but as one of Christ's body you belong.

While we cannot help our feelings with regard to religion, we are expected to do violence to them when they work against religion's realities.

Since Christianity is essentially an organism rather than an organization, Christians have constantly to remind themselves that the church is a person rather than an institution.

The church demands obedience of the faithful and for the most part gets it. When the church talks about voluntary poverty everybody looks the other way.

Why must money play so important a part in religion? It does not play so important a part in philosophy. "Well-being comes to a man" according to Epicurus, "through that which he can with dignity do without." Perhaps religious people have too exaggerated an idea of dignity.

The coat without seam was a poor man's coat. It is we who have divided it in an attempt to fit the rich.

We are all one in being insecure, inadequate, lonely, frightened, full of guilt. We are divided according to money, class, color. It seems odd that religion which does so much about the first list can do so little about the second.

———

While the finite intelligence is unable to apprehend all truth it is well able to bow before all truth. For most of us the weakness lies not in refusing such truths as we see and which seem reasonable, but in refusing to bow before all truth.

———

Religious fidelity is paying practical tribute in our daily lives to the sum of truth. We select what we feel to be reasonable. We do not go beyond what we see. Faith asks total faith.

———

The religion that is not dynamic, communicating, dies. There comes a time when ideologies cease to be causes and become labels. Communism, fascism, democracy, republicanism: these things have to be movements or they die. The same applies to our particular brand of Christianity.

———

Communism, fascism, democracy, republicanism: these things are people. Christianity is people. A way of thought has to be a way of life.

———

There is a difference between a movement and a trend. A movement is a community on the march. Trends are set *by* people; movements *are* people.

At the first pentecost Christianity was launched as an underground movement and martyrs followed. We talk about Christianity's finest age, Christianity's darkest age, the spread of Christianity, the persecution of Christianity. We are talking about Christ – "who is the same yesterday, today, the same for ever."

———

The test of all religion is primarily the test of trust and love. This is so in the problems of human existence: whether or not we respond to temporal challenges spiritually. It is all the more so in the transcendental problem of the judgment: whether or not we respond, while still in this present life, with trust and love.

THE JUDGMENT AND I

Admittedly our Lord has some solemn things to say about the judgment and hell, but he has only encouraging things to say about the Father who judges.

——————

At the judgment I shall be asked if I have loved. This will be the touchstone question. If I am not failed on this once and for all, I shall be asked further if I have believed and obeyed, accepted and trusted, prayed and followed as best I could the light that was given me.

——————

Hope notwithstanding, there can remain a lingering fear that conscience will be the chief witness to the judgment and the prosecuting counsel as well. It is a comforting thought, however, that only a bad conscience will stand condemned.

——————

Death and judgment are not risks for which we are not prepared; they are facts of which we have had no experience. Like all certainties the more we get used to them in advance the less we shall dread them.

——————

Souls are created for love, so when instead they choose to hate, they must find an environment where hate exists and where they can be in their element.

There is mention in scripture of the fire of hell. Perhaps fire here is as much symbolic as physical. Perhaps the fire results from psychological and material combustion: the man destined for heaven exploding in the confinement of hell. A soul in hell (though no evidence exists to show that there is a soul in hell) makes his own hell. Totally lacking love, and at home in hate, he cannot be anywhere else.

If our Lord tells us to be merciful as our heavenly Father is merciful it would be strange if we turned out to be more merciful than he.

"Judge not and you shall not be judged" is the text to remember in our anxieties about judgment.

We are right to talk about eternity as life after death. This shows we are not meant to think of it as death after death.

In his lifetime our Lord was even more eager to forgive sinners than to heal the sick. If we are given grace to endure what sickness there is in our lives, we can count upon being forgiven our sins whenever we ask for mercy.

Sin is more serious than sickness, the judgment more serious than the diagnosis. If we can commit ourselves so confidently to medical care we can commit ourselves to God's care with far more confidence.

Thinking imperfectly of love we think imperfectly of mercy. Since we are finite beings this is inevitable. But because God possesses an infinity of love his mercy will want to be extended infinitely.

———

Judging everything as we must in terms of time and space and quantity we cannot begin to measure mercy as it exists in God. Perhaps seeing it properly for the first time will be the judgment's greatest revelation.

———

When we are confidently assured that Judas could have been forgiven (and perhaps even, at the last moment, was) as readily as St. Peter and St. Thomas were forgiven, we pay no compliment to God's mercy by wondering if we shall be condemned at our judgment.

THE WAY AND I

Without fixed principles and total commitment I am no more than a visitor to a fairground. I am moving from sideshow to sideshow. I am on a carousel gathering speed but ending up where I started.

———

A man who knows his objective and has pledged himself to reach it by the most direct route is not bothered by alternatives any more than he is discouraged by hardship and the unexpected. He expects the unexpected and allows for it.

———

A man who has a vague idea of what is required of him is at the mercy of people stronger than himself. He is also at the mercy of his own emotions which are stronger than his will.

———

Impatience of the revealed way has been at the bottom of every heresy. Not only at the bottom of every heresy but at the bottom of every sin. Rebellion against the terms set. The will of God was put before Lucifer, Adam, Saul, Balaam, Jonah, Judas: each wanted his own kind of religion.

———

Once I come to believe that religion must suit me instead of the other way about I lose sight of God and begin to think only of my own fulfillment. Christ is no longer the way for me. I am my own way.

The way in the contemporary scene, the way for me, the way to which and to whom there must be no alternative. If Christ is not this the fault is not God's.

——————

By prayer I come to know the way not only as a principle but as a living person. Prayer binds me to the principle but lights up the person.

——————

It is easy enough, assuming we have read the gospels, to know what the way stands for. It is less easy to stand for that way ourselves. It is extremely difficult to direct our thinking and living along that way and no other.

——————

If I am sure of a fellow human being it means I can trust that person with my life. So if I am sure of a way, which in this case is a person, I can entrust my life to that way.

——————

When occasions arise of showing others the way I am not showing *my* way – which would be arrogance on my part – but Christ's. In the whole history of man there is only one person who can point to himself and say "I am the way, the truth, the life."

——————

To be committed to the way which is Christ means being committed to whatever aspects of it he may introduce me to. It will probably involve opposition and frustration and disappointment, it will possibly involve shame and guilt, it will most certainly mean the cross and obedience "even unto death."

Christ's way led up the hill of Calvary to the cross. While hanging on the cross he said, "I thirst." This is important because his is the way of thirst. So must ours be. "Blessed are they that hunger and thirst after justice" – not merely recognize it when they see it and mete it out when they have to. Christ thirsted for the justice of the Father which is also his mercy.

"I thirst." For union with the Father, for an answering love from man, for an end to misunderstanding and loneliness, for the conversion of souls, for rest and peace which could be shared with others. It was the human, divine heart thirsting and having to go dry.

God is a consuming fire, and where there is fire there is need for a corresponding element. Not that the flame should be quenched but that there should be an object to be consumed. The appropriate object here is the human heart.

UNRELATED OBSERVATIONS

The mark of the spiritually mature man is that he can endure sorrow without bitterness, bewilderment without fuss, loss without envy or recrimination or self-pity. Above all, whatever the set-backs and misunderstandings, public and private, that he maintains a belief in the essential goodness of mankind.

——————

While it is true that we believe what we want to believe, it is also true that we sometimes cannot help believing what we do not want to believe. This should give us pause.

——————

What goes for praiseworthy reserve is often only fear of being made to look foolish. A reputation for good, honest-to-God frankness is often a cover for arrogance, lack of feeling, the desire to shock.

——————

In order to disguise his inferiority a man will go to almost any lengths. In self-examination the first question might be: what am I using to shore up my self-esteem.

——————

The false attitudes which a man adopts can nearly always be traced to shame. Too afraid to face his weakness, a man will be ruthless in order to show his strength.

Most natures have their own appropriate weaknesses. The successful tend to mock, the unsuccessful to compensate, the timorous to qualify and linger on uncommitted, the sad to criticize and give up. The weakness they all have in common is the refusal to recognize the weakness.

We so hate to lose face that we will do almost anything to preserve an identity however false. The man who says he does not mind if people see through him is lying.

There is in everyone a curious mixture of self-sufficiency and self-distrust. With the one he wards off the help which he cannot well do without; with the other he enters into a hollow place of failure. If indulged, the two tendencies can produce the same result: alienation.

It is a sad fact that people who once were prayerful and have given it up are hardly conscious of what they have lost. Life goes on as before. Other interests have taken the place of prayer. Husband and wife can drift apart in the same way, beginning new lives and not missing one another. It can only mean that in marriage as in prayer the element lacking has been faith.

Standing before God the only thing we have to offer him is ourselves. And the extraordinary part is that this is exactly what he wants.

Making an elaborate list, we can put down every sort of sacrifice which we would want offered to us if we were God. When God throws away the list we cannot understand why.

God who has all asks of us just one thing. It is always that one thing which we want to keep for ourselves.

Essentially the service of God is not the piling up of practices, resolutions, prayers and penances. It is going deeper into what we have already got.

The giving of self to the service of God is not like making a single offer, handing over a single gift, receiving a single acknowledgment. It is a continued action, renewed all the time.

Even in human affairs nothing is more tedious than having to wait. In the spiritual life it can be the whole sacrifice.

Our hold on the spiritual life is so fleeting and the movement so elusive that any sort of intelligible evidence as to its condition is not to be expected. It is the way of faith after all.

How well or how badly the spiritual life is going is such an inward thing that speculation about it brings virtually no findings. Love has gone underground and to try digging it up is a mistake. Dug up it would suffer from overexposure.

To emphasize the doctrine of moderation in all things is to end up with mediocrity in all things. In Christianity's best periods the call has been frankly for heroism. Not for heroics but for heroism.

Christianity thrives on heroic sacrifice. Hence the martyrs. You cannot have a slight case of suicide. Christianity cannot be slightly sacrificial, slightly martyred, any more than today can be slightly Monday or Easter slightly Easter.

To the man of commonsense religion, with "nothing in excess" for his rule, our Lord's forty days fast in the wilderness must seem dangerously excessive. Such a man would have cautioned our Lord against exaggeration.

In the matter of vocation to the religious life the primary object is the love of a person, Christ. It is possible to think of it impersonally and in the abstract. It is then a career like any other and not a call.

People in the world herd together to work as members of an organization. In the religious life people herd together as members of an organism. There is a difference between a company and a community. A corporation is made up of separate units. A community is a unity in its own right.

It would be as absurd for a man of prayer to choose whether to be an ascetic or a mystic as it would be to choose to see out of one eye rather than out of the other, or to walk with one leg rather than with the other.

A man reads a passage from the gospel and it suddenly becomes alive. He concludes he has been granted the charism of interpreting the scriptures. It would be better if he accused himself of not having taken the trouble before to see what the passage meant.

So long as we are ready to retreat from time to time into a solitude where the proportions can come into focus we are not likely to fall into the more serious mistakes which beset religiously minded people. One of the mistakes is to think we have no need of solitude and silence.

Looking back over our lives most of us would have no difficulty in picking out the things that have given us the greatest pleasure and the greatest sorrow. More difficult would be to account for why they affected us in the way they did.

The occasions of happiness which stand out in the memory are hardly ever those to which we had looked forward. Unrelated to significant events and almost always prompted by affection, our moments of joy came as a surprise and left before we had time to get used to them.

——————

While we can be joyous without knowing why and sad without knowing why, sorrow more often than joy is occasioned by particular happenings. Partings, deaths, changes of one sort or another. Shock apart, they did not surprise us with their unhappiness at the time and do not surprise us now.

——————

While joy can be sparked off suddenly, and by something as trivial as a child's laugh, sadness can come down upon us gradually so that only after a time do we find ourselves wrapped in it.